IMAGE COMICS Presents

JACOB SEMAHN
creator/writer

JORGE CORONA
creator/artist

STEVE WANDS
inker/letterer

GABRIEL CASSATA
colorist

MORGAN BEEM
watercolorist

KATHLEEN MACKAY
editor

image

GONERS: WE ALL FALL DOWN, volume 1. First Printing. APRIL 2015. Originally published in single magazine form as GONERS #1-6. Published by Image Comics, Inc. Office of publication: 2001 Center Street, Sixth Floor, Berkeley, CA 94704.
ISBN: 978-1-63215-283-1

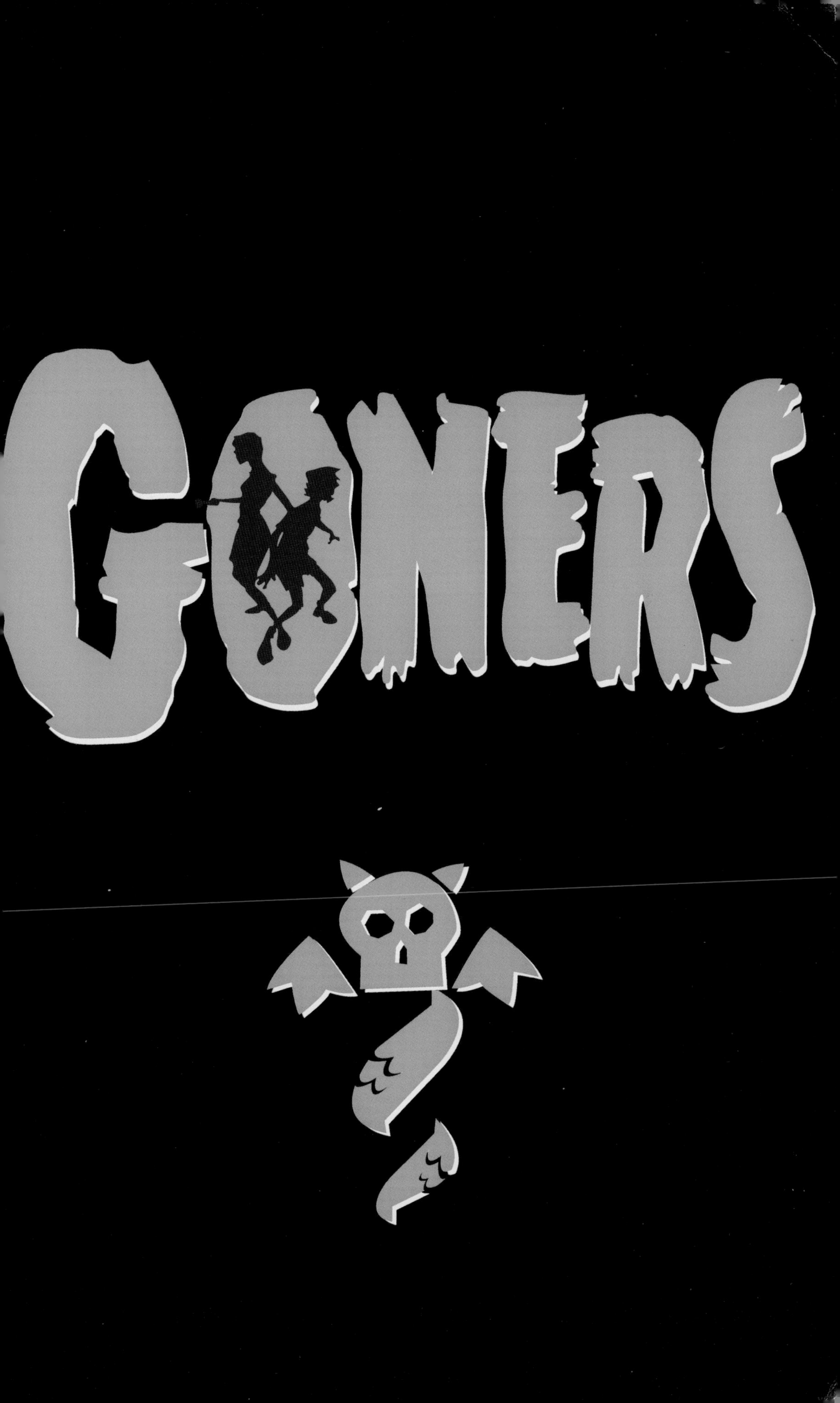
GONERS

THE
FAMILY
LATIMER.

FTER THE BEGINNING.
My first memory was written on a wall.
With absolutely no concept of a prior life...even death had eluded me--
--Until now.
"Quovis."
The word had a striking familiarity. Something that itched the back of my brain.
QUOVIS
"To whatever place you will."
Stale and cobwebbed memories flood through.
Latimer--
The writing is on the wall.

KLIP
KLOP
KING'S BLUFF, MA.
--ROBERT, I HAVE JUST ARRIVED AT THE GOVERNOR'S MANSION--
--WHERE I'VE BEEN TOLD THE FAMOUS HUNTERS, RALEIGH AND EVELYN LATIMER--FOLLOWED BY THEIR TNS CREW--HAVE ENTERED MOMENTS AGO.

IT'S ALLEGED THAT A POSSIBLE HOSTAGE TAKEOVER IS UNDERWAY. COORDINATED BY THE RADICAL MILITIA GROUP "BROTHERHOOD OF ANUBIS."
TIME FOR BED, HALF-PINT.
JOSIAH, YOU'RE TWELVE. I'M SEVENTEEN. I WIN THIS CONVERSATION... EVERY. TIME.
IS THAT THE TOASTER?
FIVE MINUTES, ZOE! THEY'VE ALMOST GOT THE PACK CLEARED!
KRASH
OH MY--! THE BODY...CARL ZOOM! GET THE BODY--!
SORRY TO INTERRUPT, PAMELA. BREAKING NEWS...AS OF 10:53 GOVERNOR CASSIUS MONTECLAN HAS BEEN DECLARED DECEASED BY EMERGENCY OFFICIALS.
AND IN A SHOCKING TWIST...EVELYN LATIMER LITERALLY HANGS ON FOR DEAR LIFE.
MOM?

TEN YEARS AGO.
MOM?
OVER HERE, HUN! C'MERE...YOU HAVE TO SEE THIS!
WHAT IS IT?
IT'S YOU, BABY GIRL.
ME?
YOU LOOK SAD.
SAD?
YOU HAVE TEARS.
OH, THOSE?
THOSE ARE HAPPY TEARS, BABY.
TEARS CAN'T BE HAPPY.
IT TAKES ALL KINDS.

RALEIGH!

ONE SECOND, HONEY!
OH...TAKE YOUR TIME! (NO PROBLEM.)

HELLO?
YOU DOUBTED?
JUST A SKOSH.
YOU SHOULD KNOW-- HNKK*

?!

'LEIGH!

'LEIGGHHHHH!!!

DAD!
NO!
CRICKKKK
DE--D--
D-DEFAECO...
RMMMBLLLL

KRACKK-THOOM
WHAT THE SHIT?!

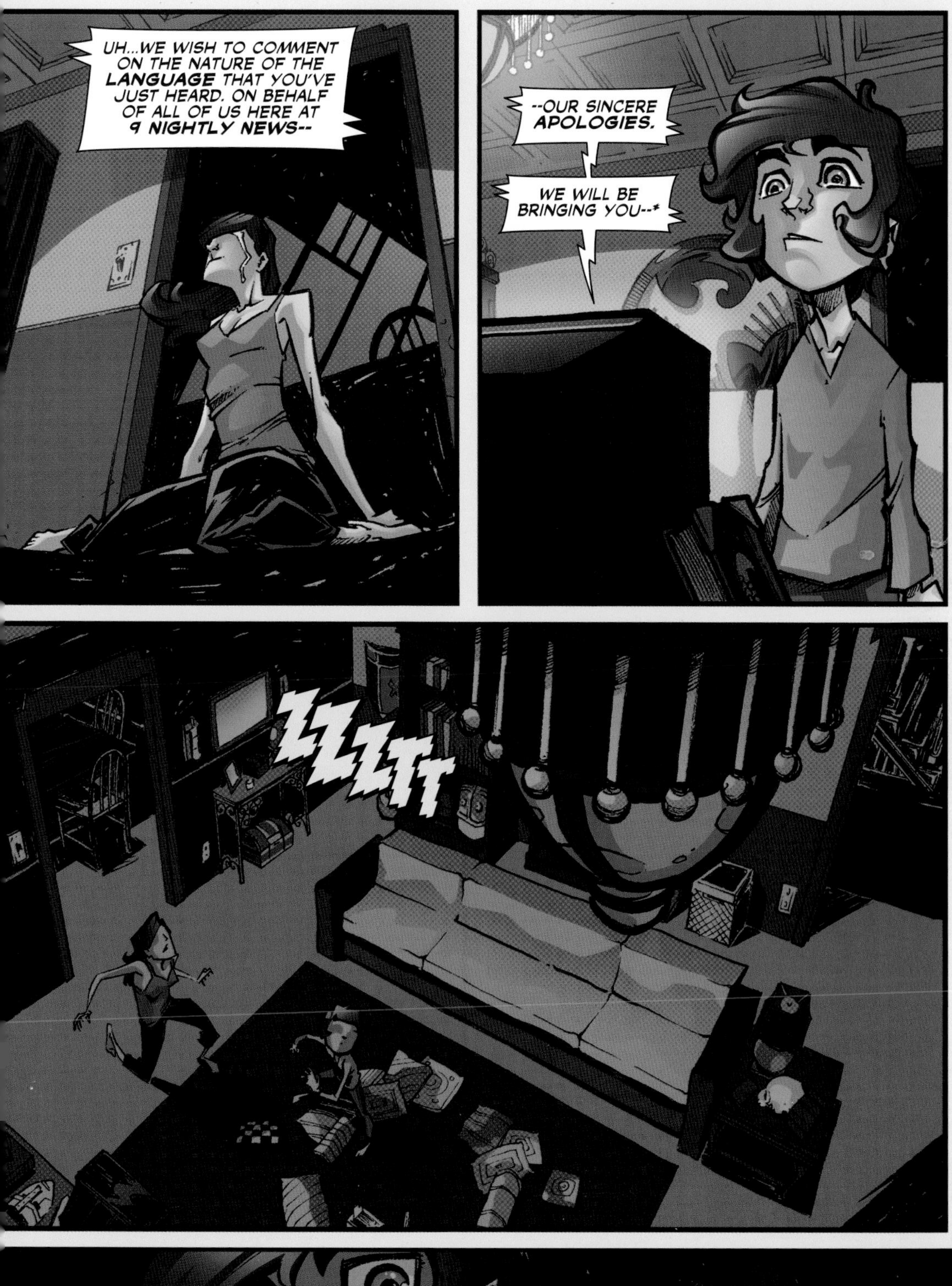
UH...WE WISH TO COMMENT ON THE NATURE OF THE LANGUAGE THAT YOU'VE JUST HEARD. ON BEHALF OF ALL OF US HERE AT 9 NIGHTLY NEWS--
--OUR SINCERE APOLOGIES.
WE WILL BE BRINGING YOU--*
ZZZZTT

KRAAK

FRANCIS?
FRANCIS? PLEASE...
RATTLLL...
CRICKKK...
RATTLLL...
GUUUHH...
AGHHHH!!

--I WANT THE ENTIRE SCENE CORDONED OFF!
COMPLETE LOCKDOWN! TURNER. HENDERSON. CROWD CONTROL! FARADAY--WHERE'S-- OKAY...FARADAY, YOU'RE POINT!
GENTLEMEN, THIS HAS TURNED INTO THE NINTH CIRCLE OF HELL! DO IT RIGHT. DO IT BY THE BOOK!
IS THAT--?
DAMN.
IT'S EVELYN.
DAMN STRAIGHT.
HAVE YOU SEEN ANYTHING LIKE THIS?
LIKE THIS?
NO.
DETECTIVE LYLE MCCARTHY?
I'M SPECIAL AGENT TULLIVER AND THIS IS SPECIAL AGENT GARRISON. FBI.
WE ARE NOW IN POSSESSION OF THIS--
PLEASE. TAKE.
LORD KNOWS I NEED A DRINK.

YOU.
WITH ME.
FRAAAAANCIS!
HAFF--!
HUFF--!
CRAATTLL... CCRITCHHH...
RATTLLL...
URGGGHH...
BOOM
RITTCH--*
CRATTCHH...
BOOM
BOOM
GUUH--?
UGGRRH?
UGRAA!
RUUH--?

GAHHH!
GAHHH!
THOOM
GARRR--*
KRAK
WRONG HOUSE.
WRONG FAMILY.
GUHHH?!
KRU-
AKKK
GARAGHH!

SORRY.
WAS CATCHIN' SHUT EYE...
FRANCIS--

T-THEY'RE-- ≻SNIFF≺
SHH...IT'S ALRIGHT, KID.
ZOE, WHAT'S GOIN' ON?

MOTHER--!

PULL UP AND HOLD BACK, WHILE I BREAK THE--

WHUMP
HOLY--!
DAMMIT!

WHAT THE HELL, FRANK?!
DIDN'T SEE YA, LYLE.
SHOULD ADD MORE FLASHING LIGHTS TO THE ROOF.

MIND FILLING ME IN TO WHAT'S GOING ON?
LOOKS LIKE A BAKAAK ATTACK--
CAN'T SPELL "DETECTIVE" WITHOUT "DETECT."
TRY SAYING THAT THREE TIMES FAST.
RUSTLE

WHAT ABOUT THE WINEAGARD ENCHANTMENT--
BANG
SORRY.
I-I--JOSIAH. ZOE.
I REGRET TO INFORM YOU THAT THERE'S BEEN AN INCIDENT.
I'M SORRY, BUT YOUR PARENTS HAVE PASSED.
SNIFF
WHAT DO--WHAT DO YA MEAN, LYLE?!
DEAD. I MEAN DEAD. AND IF I'M RIGHT, THEN THIS HOME INVASION ISN'T A COINCIDENCE. WE NEED TO GET THE KIDS OUT.
NOW.
"WHERE'S ZOE?"

TEN YEARS AGO.
ON THAT DAY MY HEART WAS FULL.
YOU FILLED IT.
THAT'S WHAT MAKES THE TEARS COME?
EXACTLY.
SINCE THAT DAY, AND FOR ALL DAYS, WE REMAIN HERE.
A PIECE OF US ALL.

WHAT ARE YOU DOING?
I CAN'T FIND IT. IT'S GONE...
THEY'RE GONE...AREN'T THEY, FRANCIS?
I-I...I'M SORRY.
WE HAVE TO GO, ZOE.
WE HAVE TO.
I'M SCARED, FRANCIS.
I KNOW, ZOE. TRUTH BE TOLD...
...I AM TOO.

KING'S BLUFF POLICE DEPARTMENT
THE INVESTIGATOR'S REPORT INDICATES THAT MONTECLAN'S NECK WAS BROKEN--CRUSHED--BEFORE THE FALL.
KING'S BLU
POLICE DEPARTM
AND ACCORDING TO THE TRAJECTORY, HIS BODY WAS USED TO KNOCK EVELYN OUT THE WINDOW.
WHAT ABOUT 'LEIGH?
SCORCHED ASH ON WOOD...
GROAN AH, HELL, 'LEIGH...
LOOK FRANK, WE GOT PIECES OF YOUR EMPLOYER IN THE MORGUE--
THEIR CHILDREN ATTACKED AT HOME--
AND TO TOP OFF THIS HELLISH HAT TRICK, WE GOT THE WINDEAGARD ENCHANTMENT LIFTED AFTER RALEIGH'S DEATH. MAKING SUCH AN ATTACK POSSIBLE--
DON'T LIKE WHERE THIS IS GOING.
NEITHER DO I.
THE SMELL ON THIS REEKS OF "INSIDE JOB."

DO YOU KNOW ANYONE THAT WOULD WANT TO SEE HARM DONE TO--
I DIDN'T EVEN KNOW THE LATIMERS WERE DEAD UNTIL--!
FRANK. RELAX. EVEN IF I WAS SOLD ON YOU, THIS IS A FEDERAL MATTER. SO FOR NOW I MAKE LIKE PONTIUS PILATE.
FOR A GUY THAT'S WASHED HIS HANDS, YOU SEEM VERY INVOLVED.
SUCKER FOR THE PULPS...SUE ME.
DETECTIVE McCARTHY
HMMM...
FROM THE INSIDE? EZRA JONES.
LEAD TACTICIAN FOR THE LATIMERS?
LET THE DRUNK GO A MONTH AGO. DIDN'T GO SO HOT.
GOTCHA. ONE LAST THING.
HOW MANY BAKAAKS STORMED THE MANOR?
AND YET, PROBABLY NOT.
NOKK NUH NOK NOKK

FBI REPORT YOU REQUESTED, SIR.
DANKE, HENDERSON.
OH AND SIR... COMMISH NEEDS YOU TO SIGN AND LOG REESE ADMOR'S AUTOPSY REPORT ASAP.
BOY, IT'S JUST RAINING SHIT TODAY...I'LL TAKE CARE OF IT.
ADMOR?
AS FOR BAKAAKS...
...THERE WERE, I DUNNO, A DOZEN. WHY?
BECAUSE EVERYONE, BUT THE LATIMER TACTICAL SQUAD, HAVE BEEN ACCOUNTED FOR.
THEY POOF... VANISHED.
FBI
AND THEY WERE ALL OF TWELVE STRONG.

ADMOR... ADMOR...
MORE OF WHAT?
ADMOR... ADMOR...
Madam Admor
1313 Trafalgar Place
King's Bluff, MA
MADAM ADMOR!
I hope this reaches you in time
It is a matter of the strictest urgency.
Love, ~ R.
WE NEED TO FIND DAD'S LETTERS!
WE NEED TO FIND EZRA JONES.
ZEEE-OHHHWWW

OH, C'MON! THIS IS GETTING OLD!
TACTICAL ADVANTAGE.
THEY SEE BEST IN THE DARK.
I HEARD SKITTERING!
GET BEHIND SOMETHING.
GET BEHIND ME.
SERIOUSLY?
WHAT? I DON'T HAVE A MUSKET LYING AROUND.
WE'LL HAVE TO MAKE DUE UNTIL O.W.A.T. ARRIVES.
DO ME A FAVOR. TURN ON THOSE BABY GREENS AND TELL ME "WHO COMES KNOCKING AT MY DOOR."
SCRNOK...KRONOFK...

IT'S HENDERSON.
I LOCKED THE DOOR! HE'S TRAPPED!
DUNNO ABOUT THAT...
CLONK... KNACKK...
DETECTIVE McCARTHY
"...THAT'S NOT HENDERSON'S KNOCK.
SCRIFF... SCHNOK...

JORGE
COR
2014

P.W.

HRRRMMMMMM...

VALON BAY, MAINE.
LIGHT'S OUT.
AFTER YEARS OF THE SAME OLD TUNE, THIS BEAT NEVER GETS OLD.
HEH.

RAIN'S COMING. COURSE IT IS...JUST GOT THE DAMNED CAR WASHED.

HOPE THEY DECORATED. STREAMERS AND RIBBONS...
...AND BALLOONS!

BALLOONS...OH, HOW I LOVE--

AAAAAIEEE!
Everything.
Everything she has ever known.
TED?! OH--!

MY... OH--OH, MY GOD!
MY BABIES!

MY... OHHH--*
Her world goes black.
Gail Turtletaub. Forty-five today--
Happy Birthday Mom!
--maiden name: Latimer.

IN A DIFFERENT PLACE.
--WHERE THIS DRAMATIC--
--STORY CONTINUES TO UNFOLD.
<TRULY A GRISLY SIGHT TO-->*
*TRANSLATED FROM RUSSIAN. ED.
<--AS WE LEAD UP TO THE FOURTH HOUR OF A FAMILY, TRULY UNDER SIEGE.>*
*TRANSLATED FROM FRENCH. ED.

RUNNING LOW, FRANCIS!
ONE. DON'T CALL ME, FRANCIS! TWO...
KA-BOOM
...IF ANYONE IS GONNA END ME, IT'S DEFINITELY NOT THESE PALE ASSHOLES!
CLEAR A PATH, MEN! MAKE AN EXIT--!

EKEK!
--AND FARADAY! WHERE ARE MY NIGHT LIGHTS?!
HNN--!
TWO MINUTES, MCCARTHY!
EKEKEKEK!
BLAM
BLAM
AGGHHHH!!
ALBERTO-- OH MY GOD!
GOD?! THERE IS NO GOD--! RUN FOR YOUR LIVES!
BOOM
GRRRRRRR!

AH, SHIT!
LYLE!
FRANK, GET THESE KIDS OUT OF HERE!
ON IT-- ARGH!
CRAP!
FRANCIS!
RUN!

GRARRRR!
NO-- AHHH! ARGH!
BLAM

CLOSE YOUR EYES, KID.
I GOT YOU.
FOR CHRISSAKES--!

MOVE!

OHMYGOD! OHMYGOD!OH MYGOD!
I WANT DAD!
QUIET!I'M SAVINGYOUR LIFE!
HHSSS!
HNNNH?!
ZOE!
STRIKING NIGHT LIGHT!
SKREEEEE!
JOSIAH! C'MON!

HOLY SHIT--! WE MADE IT?!

DOWN--!

NOW--!

FIRE!
KA-BOOM
BLAM
KA-BOOM
BLAM
BLAM
KA-BOOM

I DON'T WANT...I DON'T WANNA DIE.
SHH...
THINK OF HAPPY. THINK OF HOME...

CLINK
CLINK

CLINK
CLINK

FIVE YEARS AGO.
--ANNNND THREE BECOME ONE!
CLAP! CLAP! CLAP!
THANKS! THANK YOU!
NO REALLY... YOU'RE TOO KIND.
OKAY SURE. KEEP IT COMIN'.

NOW FOR MY NEXT TRICK...
...I REQUIRE A VOLUNTEER.

ET THE KIDS HAVE THEIR FUN, HANK.
ALMOST HAVE THIS DAMNED CHARADE FIGURED OUT.
I CAN CRACK IT THIS TIME!

JOSIAH!
HUH?

YOU'RE TOO OLD UNCLE HANK!
TOLD YOU.
ONLY CAUSE SHE KNOWS I'M ONTO HER GAME.
I GOT YOUR NUMBER, SWEET-HEART.

JOSEY, PICK A CARD! ANY CARD!
GO 'HEAD AND SHOW THE CARD OFF.
NOW SLIP THE CARD BACK IN THE DECK, ANYWHERE... DOESN'T MATTER.
AND WITH THE POWER OF MY MIND'S EYE, I WILL SUMMON YOUR CARD FORTH!
IT'S CALLED MAGIC, FOLKS! ONLY THE MOST DISCIPLINED CAN MASTER IT!
CHIN CHIN!
GROAN
STOP BEING BITTER.
I HOPE YOU KNOW THAT SHE TAKES HER CHEAP THEATRICS FROM YOU.
BITTER.
BY A GAME OF TRICKS?
SLEIGHT OF HAND.
WHATEVER.

IS THIS YOUR CARD?!
Y--YES.
OF COURSE IT IS!
THE AMAZING Z NEVER FAILS TO HIT HER MARK!
MAGIC IS A MERE PLAYTHING TO ME! HA HA!
CLAP! CLAP! CLAP!

TERRY! JESSE! C'MON, I SMELL HOTDOGS!
HOTDOGS!
I NEED TO FRESHEN MY DRINK. HANK?
BE OUT IN A SEC.
LOVE YOUR TIE, TED. IS IT SILK?
NO.
WELL... MAYBE?

UNCLE HANK? WAS THAT REAL? LIKE, REAL MAGIC?
HEY, HALF-PINT.
OH, C'MON...PLEASE TELL ME YOU WERE NOT SHOCKED AND AWED BY THIS.
YOU WEREN'T IMPRESSED?
HARDLY. THEATRICAL? YES. IMPRESSED? NOT SO MUCH AFTER WHAT I'VE SEEN.
BESIDES, MAGIC JUST LIKE EVERYTHING IN LIFE, IS A SERIES OF ONE ILLUSION...
...AFTER ANOTHER.
WOW. REALLY? SHE BOUGHT FIFTY-TWO DECKS?

BUT LET'S GET BACK TO YOUR PARTY. WHAT ARE YOU NOW? EIGHT?
SEVEN.
UNCLE HANK? YOU'RE PRETTY COOL.
YEAH...
...I AM PRETTY DAMNED COOL.

COME ON--!
COME ON--!
COME ON--!
JOSEY?
JOSEY?
C'MON, KID!
JOSIAH!
WUZZAT?
C'MON! WE GOTTA JET, KID! UP!
(CAN'T BELIEVE YOU FAINTED.)
SHUT IT, ZOE.
YOU GOOD?

A-OKAY.
WATCH YOUR STEP. THERE ARE BODIES EVERYWHERE.
JUST WANNA GET OUT OF HERE.
AND THAT'S EXACTLY WHAT WE'RE DOIN', ZOE.
?
"DEATH ISN'T SOMETHING TO BE AFRAID OF..."
...IT'S WHAT MAKES LIFE WORTH LIVING.
PLUS...I BELIEVE THE NEXT GREAT ADVENTURE RESIDES IN THE BEYOND.
BUT--WHAT IF THERE'S NOTHING WHEN YOU DIE?

"WELL THEN, THE JOKE WOULD BE ON ME, WOULDN'T IT?"
HNNK

BLAAARFF!

HE PUKED ON ME, DIDN'T HE?

GROAN
UH? MIXED WITH ALL THAT BLOOD, IT'S... NOT THAT BAD?
(GROSS)
GONNA MAKE IT?
THINK SO...

GUYS, WE REALLY NEED TO STAY SHARP AND GET MOVING FOR--
--QUIET!

I THOUGHT I HEARD SOMETHIN'.
DON'T HAVE A VISUAL ON ANYTHING DOWN--
GET BACK--!
PLIP
SKREEEE!
BLAM BLAM
BLAM
BLAM
AHHH!
AH, MOTHER--!
THINK I JUST BLEW MY GODDAMN EARDRUM!

SKREEEE!
GO, GET OUT OF HERE.
YOU!
STICK AROUND!
SKRIT--?
GRARR!
RRGG!
WARGS, INCOMING!
GOD I HOPE YOU'RE LOADED.
KA-BOOM
KLIK
GET TO SAFETY!
I GOT THIS!

RAAARR!
AHHH!
SKRIK
DAMMIT ALL...WHERE ARE YOU?
ARGH... THERE YOU ARE.
RRRRRR
HRRRG...
RAAAAAAH!
GDAAR--*
KRAK

--WRACHHH!
SHLOPP
KLOP
SHLUMP

WRACHHH!
SOMEONE'S GOT ISSUES. JESUS...

GRRRRRR...

MY, WHAT *HUFF* BIG TEETH *HUFF* YOU HAVE...

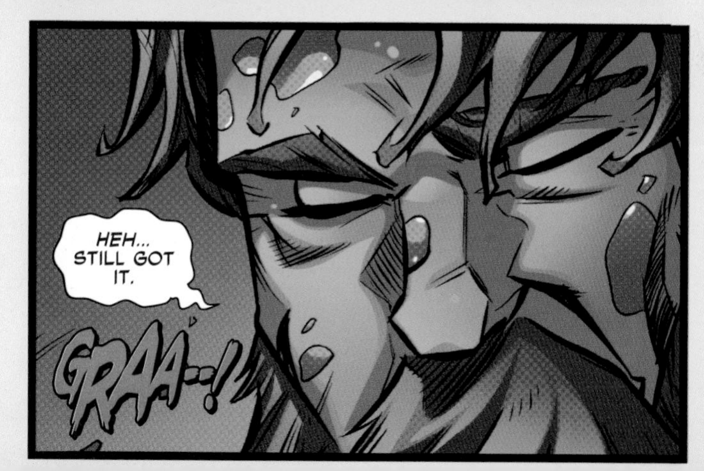
HEH... STILL GOT IT.
GRAA--!

--AAWR!
SNAP
BET THAT SMELLS LOVELY.

WE NEED TO GET SOME AIR!

OOOF! WHAT DO YOU--?!
KIDS...!
...DON'T TENSE UP!

EK!
EK!
WHAT ARE YOU *TALKING--?!*
OH NO NONONONO... YOU'RE NOT GOING TO LIKE IT.
NO.
WAY.
FRANCIS?
HOLD THAT THOUGHT!
YOU'RE GONNA WANNA *CLOSE* YOUR EYES FOR THIS!
TRUST ME!
NONONO NONONONONO NONONO!
FRANCIS, THAT'S A WINDOW. FRANCIS?
FRANCIS--!!
KSSSSSH
--I HAAAAATE YOUUUUUUUUUU!

I SO NEED A VACATION...

JORGE COR 2014

TENTACLES & THREADS TO STITCH HIMSELF TOGETHER?
RALEIGH'S BURNED HAND
GLOVE STILL HERE

HOW MANY?
ALL OF THEM...
...AND SOMEHOW-- SOMEWAY--SANTA ANNA WAS ABLE TO WRANGLE CHENOO TO HIS SIDE.
CHENOO? PFEH. AS IF THE BARRAGE OF IRON DAY AND NIGHT WAS NOT ENOUGH...YOU BRING ME THE IMPOSSIBLE.
I THINK WE CAN CEASE WITH DRAMATICS, WILLIAM.
WHY SUSPECT THE IMPOSSIBLE, WHEN YOU CAN LOOK FOR YOURSELF, JAMES? I UNDERSTAND LITTLE OF YOUR NEED TO DOUBT ME EVERY STEP OF--
ENOUGH. TIME IS SCARCE AND WILLIAM SPEAKS TRUE.
SANTA ANNA'S MADE PEACE WITH THE CHENOO. THEY TAKE IN WITH HIM.
DEAD MEN ALL.
REMOVE ME FROM THIS LEDGE, GEORGE. PUT ME TO WORK...

...FOR THERE WILL BE PLENTY OF *BODIES* TO FEED ON COME *SUNRISE.*

NOT A DAY PASSES THAT I DO NOT SEEK AN **END** TO YOU, MONSTER!
COME NOW...THAT *ALL* YOU SEEK, GEORGIE?
THAT AND...
...QUIET!

Hrkk--!
THUNK

TOO TIRED FOR THAT CUSSED DEVIL--
MAYBE LATIMER'S TARNAL MONSTER IS RIGHT. FIGHT FIRE WITH FIRE...
...DEVIL WITH DEVIL.
DAVY. PLEASE LISTEN. THE FOUL BEAST UNDER MY CARE YIELDS NOTHING GOOD.
AN ALBATROSS ABOUT MY NECK. I BEG YOU...TREAD LIGHTLY.
WE LIVE IN A WORLD OF FOUL BEASTS. YOUR FAMILY KNOWS FULL WELL OF THESE FACTS...BUT IN THIS MOMENT, I LEAN TO MY EXPERIENCE.
"BE ALWAYS SURE YOU'RE RIGHT...THEN GO AHEAD."
HAHAHAHA...
LOVELY SHOT. JAMES. COULD REALLY USE THAT THROWING ARM...
...TOO BAD YOU'RE ROTTED THROUGH WITH CONSUMPTION. THE SMELL OF DEATH HANGS OVER YOU...THE SMELL OF DEATH HANGS OVER US ALL.
BETTER THE DEVIL YOU KNOW...

"...THAN THE DEVILS YOU DON'T."
5:33 AM - MARCH 6, 1836.
THE ALAMO MISSION.

KING'S BLUFF POLICE STATION.
NOW.
LET ME THROUGH!
ARE THEY DEAD?! ARE THE LATIMERS DEAD?!
THEIR MAN SERVANT KILLED THEM--!
EVERYONE! BACK! GET--!
FWASH
FSHH
FLSHH

⁑GASP!⁑
⁑KOFF--!⁑
⁑KAFF--!⁑

JOSIAH! ZOE!
WHAT HAPPENED? IN YOUR OWN WORDS-- HEY! WATCH THE HANDS, PAL!

WHAT ARE YOU FEELING RIGHT NOW?!
WITH YOUR PARENT'S BRUTAL MURDER, WHAT'S NEXT FOR THE FAMILY LATIMER?!
HAS TNS CONTACTED YOU ABOUT A TWELFTH SEASON RENEWAL?!

IS HE-- IS JOSIAH LATIMER PISSING HIS--?
I--I--
GET--

SNAP

W--WHO ARE YOU?
CHRIST... THERE'S ONLY SO MUCH ONE CAN TAKE BEFORE ONE STEPS IN.
"FEED"? WHAT'S WRONG WITH THEM?
TOILET
MAKEUP
FEED
HOW ARE YOU DOING THIS?
AN EXPLANATION EXISTS...LONG AND DRAWN OUT, I'M SURE. BUT ANSWERING SUCH THINGS TAKES A CERTAIN MAGIC OUT OF IT.
AND FOR NOW, YOU MAY CALL ME SWIFT...AS IN "UNEXPECTED."
WHY ARE YOU LOOKING AT ME LIKE THAT?
WHAT DO THE WORDS ON THE FOREHEAD MEAN?
MUCH LIKE THE EXCLAMATION AT THE END OF A SENTENCE, IT INDICATES A SURPRISE.
PIERCE
JOSIAAAAH... W--WHAT'S ON MY FOREHEAD?
I OWE YOUR FATHER A SINGLE FAVOR AND CONSIDERING YOUR TIME LEFT, I FIGURED NOW IS AS GOOD A TIME AS ANY TO COLLECT.
PIERCE
HEY "DEUS EX MACHINA"! IF YOU'RE WHO I THINK YOU ARE, WHY NOT JUST SAVE US ALREADY?!
TT OH...I'M SORRY, CHILDREN. YOU HAVE IT QUITE WRONG.
I GIVE YOU A CHANCE AT CLOSURE AND MEANING...A HEAD START IS WHAT I BUY YOU. THIS IS NO TIDY RESOLUTION...

"...FOR I DON'T OWE YOUR FATHER *THAT* BIG OF A FAVOR."
SNAP
--SELF!
--AWAY!

FRANK? THEY'RE *GONE...*
...THE *KIDS* ARE GONE.

TWELVE YEARS AGO.

SOMETHIN' TO WARM YA, SIR?
WHILE I CAN APPRECIATE THE SENTIMENT, FRANCIS. THIS IS A *POOR TIME.*

INDEED, SIR. THANK YOU, SIR. IF THAT WILL BE ALL--
NO. WAIT.
WHEN WE NEEDED YOU...WHAT WE MADE YOU FOR--
THE LATIMER RITUAL OF CREATION IS A GREAT DEFENSIVE TRADITION THAT HAS BEEN PASSED DOWN FOR GENERATIONS. MOST EXCEL, WHILE FEW DO NOT.
I'M NOT ONE TO BEAT AROUND BUSHES... YOU'VE FAILED FRANCIS. THE DEMON ALMOST LAID CLAIM TO MY MOST PRIZED POSSESSION AND YOU WERE WHAT--?
I--I WAS IN TWILIGHT--
YOU WERE SLEEPING. ON THE JOB.
SHE ALMOST GOT HIM...
...SHE ALMOST GOT JOSIAH, FRANCIS.
DO NOT FAIL US-- FAIL ME-- AGAIN.
DO YOU UNDERSTAND?
YES, SIR. SORRY, SIR.
IF YOU'RE NOT BUSY DYIN', LYLE. WE GOTTA MOVE.
I GOT CHILDREN TO PROTECT.

WHY WORRY ABOUT MONSTERS, WHEN YOU CAN KILL US YOURSELF?!
JUST EASE OFF THE GAS! THERE ARE TWO PEDALS Y'KNOW?
STOP YELLING! NOT MY FAULT I WASN'T TAUGHT HOW TO DRIVE!
VROOM
SKI-EEECH
USE THAT EIDETIC MEMORY OF YOURS... THIS LOOK FAMILIAR TO YOU? NEVER TAKEN THE BACK ROADS.
YEAH. JUST AROUND THE BEND.
AND WHAT ARE WE DOING? WHAT ARE WE SUPPOSED TO BE LOOKING FOR?
ANSWERS.
OKAY. STOP BEING CRYPTIC. THIS ISN'T SOME DIME-STORE MYSTERY NOVEL. COUGH IT UP, HALF-PINT.
I--I...
...I THINK DAD WAS HAVING AN AFFAIR.
DON'T BE AN ASSHOLE. DAD WAS NOT--
ZOE! LOOK OUT!
HOLY--!
SCREECH
J2S-GK

VRRRRRRRR
KSSSSH
SMAAAASH
KOFF
NEVER DRIVING WITH YOU AGAIN...
NEVER DRIVING AGAIN... PERIOD.
WHAT WAS THAT THING?
DIDN'T GET A GOOD LOOK... SASQUATCH?
HEY LOOK... THE MANOR'S JUST BEYOND THE CLEARING. LET'S HOOF IT.
WAIT. LEMME GRAB A FLASHLIGHT.
OH HO! AND WE SHOULD TOTALLY BRING THIS!
OH NONO NO.
CH-CHAK
OH YESYES YES.

"YOU SURE THIS IS THE PLACE, FRANK?"
"YEAH... I'M SURE."

"THOUGH, I'M NOT SURE YOU BROUGHT ENOUGH MEN."
"WE'LL GET BY."
CRAK

DOWN ON THE FRICKIN' GROUND! NOW!
SHHH SHHHSHH...LET'S NOT RUIN THE MOMENT.

NO!
STOP!
BACK UP NOW-- ARGH!
BLAM BLAM
SIGH
KEEP YOUR MEN...

...I'LL HANDLE THIS.
TOLD HIM IT WASN'T ENOUGH.
FRANK. WHAT AN ALTOGETHER NOT SURPRISING SURPRISE.
EZRA.
HNH... RUBBER BULLETS. MIGHTY GENTLE.
SURE WHEN THESE GUYS WAKE UP, THEY'LL BE OF LIKE MIND.
ONLY GONNA ASK ONCE, JONES... WHERE ARE THEY?
THEY'RE IN THE BACK. NOT REALLY UP FOR VISITORS RIGHT NOW...SEEING AS HOW THEY'RE STILL IN A STATE OF GRIEVING.
ONE WAY OR ANOTHER, THEY'RE COMIN' WITH ME.
AND HERE MY HOROSCOPE SAID TODAY WAS GOING TO BE A QUIET ONE...

RARGH!
BLAM
BLAM
BLAM
...THANK GOD FOR LOUD.
--KILL YOU...
KRASH
PROMISES. PROMISES.
ARGH!
OOPH!

HNRH!
WHAM
ARGH!
BLAM BLAM
YOU KNOW THE PROBLEM WITH YOU CREATIONS...YOU'RE NOT HUMAN. NOT MONSTER. NO...
YOU'RE EITHER THE PIN...
...OR THE GRENADE.
HNNN...
THEY SAY YOU CAN'T DIE...NOT CONVENTIONALLY ANYHOW.
THAT'S WHAT THEY SAY.
WELL, I SAY: "LET'S FIND OUT."
EZRA. NO.

LET HIM UP.
WE NEED ALL THE HELP WE CAN GET AGAINST HER.
WHERE ARE THE CHILDREN, FRANK?

HANK? GAIL?! THAT'S WHO YOU WERE PROTECTIN'?
CREATIONS KILLED LATIMERS BEFORE. CAN'T TRUST 'EM. AND LIKE GAIL SAID..."WHERE ARE THE CHILDREN"?
LOST 'EM. THOUGHT I'D FIND 'EM HERE.
WHAT DID YOU MEAN BY "HER"?
THE LILIN IS BACK. SHE'S COMING FOR WHAT'S HERS... AND RAZING THE REST.

JUST--! THIS IS JUST FANTASTIC.
NOW WHERE'D I LEAVE THAT BOURBON?
JOSIAH?
WHAT ABOUT YOU AND YOURS?

THEY DIDN'T--WELL... I FOUND HER IN TIME.
SOB

UH...
...EVERYBODY, FREEZE?

SO YOU THINK, WHAT? DAD'S LOVE LETTERS WILL LEAD TO WHY THEY WERE KILLED?
DUNNO. SOMETIMES...
WHY ARE YOU WHISPERING?
...THIS PLACE GIVES ME THE CREEPS.
IT'S STILL OUR HOME, ZOE. NO PLACE LIKE IT.
YOU WERE ALWAYS A LITTLE MORE ENAMORED WITH IT THAN I WAS.
DON'T LOOK AT ME LIKE THAT. I WAS FALLING OVER MYSELF TO LEARN THE FAMILY BUSINESS AT YOUR AGE TOO. TRAINED FOR TWO YEARS EVEN.
BUT YOU GROW OUT OF IT. TRUST ME. I HAVE ZERO INTEREST IN HUNTING MONSTERS. OCCULT HERO, I AM NOT.
THERE'S ANOTHER SIDE TO THIS. A DARK SIDE. ONE THAT MOM AND DAD PAINT A PRETTY PICTURE OF.
I WANT TO BE NORMAL. LIKE--
--AUNT GAIL?
BUT WE MIGHT BE ALL THAT'S LEFT...THE ONLY ONES TO CARRY ON THE FAMILY TRADITION. THEY WOULD'VE WANTED--
NO, JOSEY. BEING THE LAST...IT'S NOT HOPE...
...IT'S A DEATH SENTENCE.
GO...

"...GO LOOK FOR YOUR LETTERS.
KLIK
"...LOOK FOR THE BAD."

"WHERE ARE YOU GOING?"

"TO LOOK FOR THE GOOD."

I AM WITH HEAVY HEART AND MANY SORROWS, ZOE.

THANKS, XIAN.
≶HEH≶ YOU'RE KINDA NICE, WHEN YOU'RE NOT TRYING TO KILL ME.
IT DOES ME LITTLE GOOD IF EVERYONE THAT LIVES HERE IS DEAD.
ALTHOUGH, IF CONSUMED WITH REMORSE TOO GREAT. OVERFILLED WITH... THOUGHTS--
--YEAH, I KNOW I KNOW. DON'T WORRY...
...I'LL DO YOU A SOLID AND THROW MYSELF OVER THE BANISTER.
IT PLEASES ME TO HEAR THIS. OH, AND ZOE?
YEAH?
YOUNG JOSIAH IS BEING MURDERED UPSTAIRS.
KLIP
KLIP
KLIP
It felt like an eternity.

For such large hands.
HNNNK... Z-ZO--EEHKK...
MANY A'SCORE, SINCE MY LAST STRANGULATION...A LATIMER CHILD NO LESS. OR AS I REFER TO THEM...
THE GOOD OL' DAYS!

For such a fragile neck.
...HAAKK--*
RECOGNIZE THE HAND? YOUR FATHER'S GENTLE TOUCH? MY REWARD...
...YOUR PUNISHMENT.

Death came slow.
FOUR LITTLE INJUNS UP ON A SPREE...
...ONE KICKED THE BUCKET AND THEN--
CHI-CHAK
HUH?
GET THE HELL OFF...

BOOM
...OF MY BROTHER!

JOSEY?
NO...

--AND THEN THERE WERE THREE.

WHAT.

BOOM

DID.

BOOOOM

YOU.

DO?!
BOOM

KRASH

COMEONCOME ONCOMEON--
RIIIIP
For this is what awaits all Latimers.
HNN! HNN! NOT YET.
NOT NOW. COME ON, JOSIAH!
Not gift...
SHOOO...
...Nor curse...
HNN! HNN! HE'S JUST A KID!
PLEASE... SOB
...HE'S JUST A KID.
...But tragedy.

JORGE
COR
2014

POP!
SKINWALKER
WOLF FUR COWL
BOUND LEATHER

KING'S BLUFF COUNTY MORGUE.
ASSAULT ON KING'S BLUFF: GOVERNOR AND LATIMERS DEAD--
THEY'RE RAIDING...
AND WITH RALEIGH AND EVELYN LATIMER DEAD--
WE'RE SO SCREWED.
EH? WHATTYAGONNA DO? ALL END UP THE SAME WAY...
...DEAD IS DEAD, FAMOUS OR NOT.
ASK ME... THE LOSS OF A COUPLE OF CELEBRITIES DOES NOT AN ARMAGEDDON MAKE.
CLLK CLLK CLLK
?
WHAT'S THAT SOUND?
CLLK CLLK CLLK CLLK
MUTE
VERMONT'S TEIHIIHAN DWARF INVASION
CHEW
QUIT WIFTH THE NERVES, KID.
CHEW
YOUFH GOTTA LEARN TO EASE UPF 'ROUND THE RECENTLY...
CLLK CLLK CLLK
...DECEASED?
CLLK CLLK CL

GRARR!
AAHH!
AHHH!
NO--! NOOOOO-- ARGHHHHHH--*
GURGLE
SPLURTCH

♫
♫
KLIK
TT A RUNNER.
GROSS FEET.
GOOD FACE.
TIGHT SKIN. FINE STRUCTURE.
BEAUTIFUL.
LOAD IT UP.
SHE AWAITS.

LATIMER MANOR.
I--
WUMP
--REFUSE!
WUMP
DO YOU HEAR ME?!
I CAN'T--! NOT YOU...
...I CAN'T LOSE YOU TOO!
WAKE UP, JOSIAH!
WUMP

...

WHAT WE ATTEMPT, WE DO NOT ATTEMPT LIGHTLY...
?
...RALEIGH.
DAD?
WHAT THE HECK--?
ARE YOU CERTAIN THIS CHILD IS IN POSSESSION OF THE LILIN?
NO! WHY WON'T YOU BELIEVE ME?! WHY WON'T ANYONE BELIEVE--?!
SHH... BABY. IT'S ALMOST OVER.
--YES. I AM CERTAIN, MADAM ADMOR.
SEPH HOLDS SWAY OVER ANNETTE PRYOR. WE MUSTN'T DELAY!
GOTTA BE DREAMING.
THIS IS INSANE.
SOB PLEASE! I'M SO...SO--SCARED SOB I'M NOT IN NO SWAY...
I'M SCARED.
I'LL BE GOOD, I SWEAR!
LET HER GO! SHE'S JUST A--!
--A LITTLE GIRL?

YES. YOU ARE RIGHT...
...I WAS NOT.
D-DAD...?
DAD!
SON.
AM I-- Y'KNOW?
THAT'S... RATHER MURKY AT THE MOMENT.
WE'RE WORKING ON IT.

"WE--" MOM?
NO. WE CAN'T FIND YOUR MOTHER...
...AND FRANKLY THERE ARE MORE PRESSING MATTERS--
WHAT'S MORE IMPORTANT THAN FINDING MOM?!
FINDING YOU.
ME?! WHY--! WHY AM I HERE? WHAT IS THIS?!
THIS IS PART OF IT. A PAYMENT.
A CONFESSION...
...OF MY GREATEST SIN.
THE SIN OF IGNORANCE.
BLECH! WHAT THE--?!
WHY DO I NEED TO SEE YOU DOING THAT WITH...

...MOM?

AS I SAID-- "YOU WERE RIGHT."
THE PRYOR GIRL WAS NOT IN THE LILIN'S GRASP...

...YOUR MOTHER WAS.
AND IN TURN...
...SO WAS I.

EVELYN AND I TRACKED DOWN A CULT THOUGHT TO BE IN SEARCH OF TYPICAL WISH-FULFILLMENT FARE--RICHES, POWER, FULL HEAD OF HAIR--THE USUAL.
IT WAS MINOR. THE TRAIL. NOTHING BUT A DEAD CAT HERE. A TWO-HEADED COW THERE.
NOTHING LIKE WHAT WE FOUND THAT HELLISH NIGHT.
THE NIGHT THEY CALLED FORTH THE DEMON SEPH.
WE HUNTED THE SUCCUBUS. RELENTLESS...
...MISTAKES WERE MADE.
DO YOU UNDERSTAND WHAT I'M TELLING YOU? DO YOU GET IT?
...
W-- WHEN--? WHEN DID THIS HAPPEN?
THIRTEEN YEARS AGO.
I'M SO SORRY, JOSIAH...
HNNK
IF ONLY THERE WERE TIME FOR TEARS.
I'M DEAD... NOTHING BUT TIME.
AND I PRAY THERE IS ENOUGH OF IT TO PROPERLY PREPARE YOU.
FOR THIS ISN'T YOUR DEATH...
...IT'S YOUR TRAINING.

DAMMIT! WAKE UP, JOSIAH!
...

HUH?!

AM I...I'M-- BACK?
(OUCH.)

THE AMAZING Z NEVER FAILS TO HIT HER MARK!
HAHAHAHA!

OH GOD...I'M TOO LATE.
T-THAT'S... IMPOSSIBLE. I WHAMMO-BLAMMO, BLEW HIM APART.
HOW LONG HAVE I BEEN GONE, ZOE?
GONE?
DEAD?
DEAD.
HOW LONG?!
DUNNO...
...FIVE MINUTES?
HMM...
UHH... EARTH TO HALF-PINT?
HOW MANY BRAIN CELLS YOU KILL?
IT'S SO HARD TO HOLD ONTO... WITH EACH SECOND, I FORGET...
FORGET WHAT--?
JOSEY? WHERE YOU GOING?!
I'LL EXPLAIN ON THE WAY!
C'MON!
DUDE... WHAT THE HELL?

"JUST LET ME--NO...HAVEN'T FOUND THE LATIMER KIDDIES...PROBABLY DEAD--
"WELL, IT'S A PRETTY DAMNED GOOD GUESS IF YOU ASK ME!
"ROBERT, I NEED YOU TO LISTEN TO ME--"
EKEK!
THE KING'S BLUFF 73RD ANNUAL PUMPKIN MAZE – CANNONBALL PARK
HELP ME!
GUGGGH...
GRRRR...
NO. I HAVEN'T SEEN CARL.
THAT'S WHAT I'M TRYING TO TELL YOU. HELL HAS COME TO KING'S BLUFF.
...THE TOWN SQUARE'S BEEN RAIDED...AND I'M TALKING WIPED OUT IN A MATTER OF MINUTES!
ING

NO! I CAN'T COME BACK IN RIGHT NOW!
A SHIT TON OF WARGS AND THE KING OF TAXIDERMY ARE OUT. JUST-- Y'KNOW...?
...CASUALLY OUT FOR, LIKE, A STROLL AND SHIT. OH, BUT WITH A BODY BAG. BECAUSE WHY WOULDN'T THEY HAVE A BODY BAG?!
WELL, I'M SORRY! I SAY "SHIT" WHEN I'M ANGRY. OR HAPPY. OR--!
GRRRR...
UH... ROBERT? GONNA HAVE TO CALL YOU BACK.
WELL...
...SHIT.
GRRRR...
SNIFF
RRRAR...

GRAARDR!
YIII!
I'M TOO IMPORTANT TO DIE IN A PHONE BOOOOOTH!
♫
CLLK CLLK
CLLK CLLK CLLK
?
WHERE THE HELL--?
KRASH
AAHHHH!

ARGH!
STOP! PLEASE--! DO YOU KNOW WHO I AM--?!
SUSTENANCE.

KA-CHAK
HNN?
WHOEVER SAID THERE'S NOTHING TO DO IN KING'S BLUFF...
...WAS OBVIOUSLY NOT USING THEIR IMAGINATION.

SHOTGUN.
SHORT-SIGHTED.
SURE, IT CAN'T SHOOT SILVER...

...THAT'S WHAT THE MUSKETS ARE FOR.
NOT WEREWOLF...

EK!
EKEK!
EK!
...I'M A SKIN-WALKER!
LIGHT 'EM!
KEEP ON THEM!
BLAM
BLAM
BLAM
SNKT-BOOM
SO MUCH FOR THE ANTIQUE.
SNKT-
OWWR!
YIP!
AHHH!

EKEKEKEK!
EKEK!
BLAM
BLAM
GAHHH!
EYE ON THE BIRDIE.
NYAAH!
GARAGHH!
WE NEED REINFORCE-MENTS!
EEP!
YOU GOTTA BE FREAKING KIDDING ME!

LAST LETTER ADMOR SENT TO DAD WAS ABOUT GETTING SOME GUY NAMED GEORGE AND HIS BOOK OUT.
OUT OF WHERE?
BELLWEATHER.
'CAUSE THE NIGHT COULDN'T GET CREEPIER...
ALSO, P.S.-- TOTALLY KNEW DAD WASN'T CHEATING ON MOM.

...
YEA.
WE SHOULD BE QUIET NOW... ALMOST THERE.

JOSIAH...?
...DON'T.

ZOE? WHAT IS IT?

DON'T GO.
WHAT ARE WE EVEN DOING HERE?
I--I CAN'T--
I JUST CAN'T ANYMORE.

IT'S NOT FAIR. I'VE--WE'VE ALREADY LOST TOO MUCH.
CAN'T LOSE YOU TOO...NOT AGAIN. NOT TO WHATEVER THIS IS.
YOU HAVEN'T. NOT TO THIS.
BUT WE NEED TO FINISH IT.
WE'RE NOT HEROES, JOSIAH!
WE'RE KIDS!
THIS ISN'T ADVENTURE! THIS IS LIFE AND DEATH!
WE'RE LATIMERS! WE HAVE TO--
WHY?!
WHAT'S THE POINT...? WHAT'S IT WORTH?
IT'S WORTH EVERYTHING.
THE WORLD IS COUNTING ON US...
AND I CAN'T REMEMBER WHY...
...BUT I NEED YOU ZOE.
I NEED MY SISTER.
JOSIAH... I--
HEY--! SLOW YOUR ROLL...
...LOOK. I'M NOT LEAVING YOU--
THEN FOLLOW ME.
SIGH
JUST--
--FINE. FINE!
HEH
...PUSHOVER.

HOW WE LOOKING UP THERE, Z-1...?

STILL HAVE EYES ON THE SKIN-WALKER? THE WARGS?
COPY COPY...

...WE HAVE VISUAL.

LOOKS LIKE THE FLEABAGS ARE DRAGGING SOMETHING.

THE HELL THEY GOING?
I KNOW...

...THEY'RE HEADING TO BELLWEATHER.
THEY'RE HEADING TO THE IMMORTAL.

GAIL... DON'T START UP WITH THAT AGAIN. THE GUY'S PURE FICTION.
NO, SAW HIM ONCE...
...YOU DID TOO. WE ALL DID.

FORTY-FIVE YEARS AGO.
"WHEN WE WERE KIDS--HANK, RALEIGH, AND I--WOULD PLAY TAG IN THE FOREST SURROUNDING THE MANOR.
I SEE YOU, 'LEIGH!
NO FAIR!
HAHA! RUN 'LEIGH!
RUN!
"SURE THE FOREST WAS WILD...
"...BUT WE WERE WILDER.
I'M GONNA GIT YA!
HAHA HA!
AHHH!
LEIGH!
KRFF
RALEIGH?!
MARCO!
POLO...
OW.
HEY GUYS--! COME DOWN! TREASURE HUNT!
NRGHH...
"AND IN SOME WAYS...

"...TREASURE DID AWAIT.
"A MADMAN CHAINED TO THE WALL.
"BURIED AND ERASED FROM MEMORY."
TRICK. TREAT. FEET. MEAT.
AH! LET GO! HANK! GAIL!
MITTS OFF, PAL!
MMM. UPSET... REGRET.
"HE WAS SO SCARED... FRAIL EVEN. WHO KNEW HOW LONG HE'D BEEN CHAINED DOWN THERE?"
DON'T, GAIL.
HE'S PROBABLY HERE FOR A REASON.
WHY ARE YOU DOWN HERE?
BOOK...
"HE OPENED THIS RATTY ANCIENT BOOK, WITH ITS PAGES MADE FROM THE SUN."
"WARS FOUGHT. HEAVENS TOPPLED.
...LOOK.
"ALL OF CREATION DANCED AND DIED FOR US.
"NEXT THING I KNEW, I WAS IN BED. TIME LOST TO ME..."
THUNT

"...AS TIME WAS LOST FOR THE IMMORTAL."
BELLWEATHER SANATORIUM
LOVELY STORY. ONE I DON'T RECALL IN THE LEAST. BUT SUCCESS! TENSION'S EASED.
DO YOU ALWAYS HAVE TO BE SO CONDESCENDING?
APOLOGIES, DEAR. TEND TO GET THAT WAY WHEN MARKED FOR DEATH.
AW, CHRIST...
DON'T TALK TO ME ABOUT DEATH--!
NOT. NOW!
SORRY.
SORRY.
THERE SUPPOSED TO BE AN ECLIPSE TONIGHT?
NO. WHY?

THAT'S NO ECLIPSE--!
Z-1...!

"...GET OUT OF THERE NOW!"
KA-THOOOM
BELLWEATHER SANATORIUM EXIT - TWO MIL

WHAT THE HELL WAS THAT?
NO IDEA AND NOT OUR PROBLEM.
MAAAAN... THIS IS THE OTHER SIDE OF CRAZY.
THIS IS KRAZY WITH A "K!"
WELL, HEY, WE'RE IN A SANATORIUM.
JOSEY LISTEN TO ME...WE GOTTA GET.
WE'RE SO NOT READY FOR WHAT'S BEHIND DOOR NUMBER 666--
--WHO IS?!
DIFFERENT. NO. WORSE.
SNFF
ROTTEN.
DON'T LOOK SO HOT YOURSELF.
GOT THE BODY?
IT IS HERE.
♫
LET'S SEE IT.
HAVEN'T PROPERLY MET...
...BUT YEAH...
...THAT'S EVELYN LATIMER.

⸗GASP⸗
MOM!
YES, JOSIAH?

JORGE COR
2014

MAY AS WELL COME OUT...NOT ONE FOR BEING WATCHED.
WHAT HAVE YOU DONE, SWIFT?
BOUGHT TIME...LEAST ENOUGH TO SET THINGS RIGHT, MORTIFER.
YOU BROUGHT THE LATIMER CHILD BACK.
DO YOU UNDERSTAND THE RAMIFICATIONS?
A HALF-DEMON SOUL IS EASILY CORRUPTIBLE.
WHY DO YOU THINK SEPH IS HERE? THE LILIN HAVE WAYS AROUND SUCH THINGS.
AFTER SO MUCH DEATH IT WAS WELCOME RELIEF TO FINALLY GIVE LIFE.
GIVEN THE CENTURIES, I CONSIDER THIS MY FINEST ACHIEVEMENT.
THE DEAD ARE NOT MEANT TO BE GIVEN LIFE. MY JUDGEMENT IS PASSED.
AS MINE IS ON YOU.
I AM READY.
UNDONE
YOU WERE MY GREATEST CREATION...

...GOODBYE, SWIFT.
FWOOM

SO MANY ENDS...AND MUCH WORK TO BE DONE.

SNAP

KA-THOOOM
Z-1...! GET OUT OF THERE NOW!

"DAD...I DON'T WANT TO SEE THIS."
"RARELY WILL THE WORLD ASK ANYTHING OF YOU THAT IS 'FAIR,' JOSIAH...
"IT'S NOT THE NATURE OF IT...NOT THE NATURE OF LIFE."
"THIS IS THE FIRST STEP? TO KNOWING?"
"NO CHILD SHOULD EVER KNOW THE HORRORS THAT WE GATHER.
"I'M SORRY I DID NOT BETTER PREPARE YOU FOR THE ROAD THAT LIES AHEAD."
Welcome
TO
KING'S BLUFF
- HOME OF THE LATIMERS -
POPULATION 14,524"

LATIMER MANOR.
TWELVE YEARS AGO.
GURGG... GURRGG... GRURRRR...

"--AND THE LAST BORN, WHO WAS ALSO THE FIRST, SMOTE THE SON WHO WAS ALSO HIMSELF.
GOO... HEE...
HEE--! HEE...
"THROUGH THAT RUIN, THE RISE OF LILIN WOULD BEGIN ANEW."
AND YOU, MY YOUNG AMMON, HAVE MUCH TO--
KRATCH
STEP AWAY FROM MY SON, DEMON.
OUR SON, DEAR. ALWAYS OURS.
THEN TAKE IN THE VIEW...
KNEW EVELYN HAD A FLAW.
...WHILE YOU ARE ABLE!
ABSCAECUS!
FWAAASHH
RAAAGH!!
REGNA TERRAE, CANTATA DEO, PSALLITE CERNUNNOS--!
AMMON'S MINE! ARGHH--!
BLOOD WILL OUT, LATIMER...!

"...I WILL COME FOR HIM!"
AHHH!
HUNHH HANHH
ZIP THE RUCKUS, HALF-PINT.
'S TOO EARLY.
IT'S TOO LATE...
...MUCH TOO LATE. AND WHAT COMES NEXT...
...WE WOULDN'T WANT YOU OR GEORGIE TO MISS.
AWAKE? DELIGHTFUL. WE CAN BEGIN.
AHHHH!

HOW WE LOOKING, FRANCIS?
EHHHHH...
...DEAD BY DAWN.
SURE YOU GOT NOTHING TO WORRY ABOUT, CREATION. FINALLY BE AMONG YOUR KIND.
WHEN WILL YOU GET OFF MY BACK, EZRA?!
THE MOMENT I DON'T HAVE TO LOOK OVER MINE.
SERIOUSLY? WE'RE PARTY CRASHING HELL AND YOU TWO ARE STILL AT IT? GIVE IT A REST ALREADY...JESUS.
NOT SURE I'M UP FOR THIS, HANK. WAS NEVER GOOD WITH MAGIC AND I WAS CERTAINLY NEVER GOOD AT PLAYING LATIMER.
"BENCH-WARMERS UNITE."
GAIL?
YEAH?
SORRY FOR BEFORE... WITH THE YELLING.
ƎTTƐ PLEASE...
...THE ONLY FIGHT I'M WORRIED ABOUT IS THE ONE AHEAD OF US.

--I WANT A DOUBLE STACK ON THE SOUTHEAST ENTRANCE. FARADAY... YOU'RE POINT IF I'M DOWN.
YES, SIR.

SO THIS IS ALL WE GOT. THE TROOPS ARE "ROUNDED..."

...YOU GUYS READY?
NOT IN THE LEAST.
HAHA... NO.
NOPE.
WHAT GAIL SAID.

WELL, WE AT LEAST HAVE THE ELEMENT OF SURPRISE.
AHHH... SHIT.

(CHRIST, IT GOT DARK FAST...)
TIME TO BLOW THE LID ON THIS, BLAINE--
AIMES--
YEAH... AIM IT RIGHT HERE.
SIGH NEVER MIND.
AMID THE AFTERMATH OF WHAT SOME CALL "THE KING'S BLUFF MASSACRE," REINFORCEMENTS HAVE ARRIVED TO ROUND UP ZOE AND JOSIAH LATIMER HOLED UP IN THE SAFE-HOUSE BEHIND ME.
WE HERE AT 9 NIGHTLY NEWS--A TNS AFFILIATE--WILL BRING YOU--
--THE EXCLUSIVE FIRST INTERVIEW SINCE THE TRAGEDY THAT--
HEY! WE'RE NOT DONE YET--!
UH...
RARG--!
SHIT--!
WHY DOES THIS KEEP HAPPENING TO ME?!
AHHH!
KRASH

BLAM
BLAM
QUITE THE PHOENIX. THE TOWN THAT RISES AGAIN AND AGAIN.
CRAP!
OOF!
IT IS READY.
SHOW ME, SKIN-WALKER.
MY FINEST WORK.
FORGIVE MY APPEARANCE...
...TO HIDE FROM A DEMON YOU TAKE ITS EYE. THE KEY TO RALEIGH'S WINEAGARD ENCHANTMENT.
GASP
GONNA BE SICK.

LIKE SLIPPING ON A FAVORITE PAIR...IT FITS JUST SO.
CHILDREN, SAY "HELLO" TO MOTHER.

SPEAKING OF--GO FORTH SKIN-WALKER...AND TAKE WHAT I HAVE MADE FOR YOU.
♫

IS THAT--?
ZOE... DON'T.

LET IT GO.
LET IT GO?! BUT IT'S MOM!
IT'S NOT HER...JUST A SHELL.
RATTLLL...
CRICKKK...
RATTLLL...

IT'LL DRIVE YOU MAD. IT'LL MAKE YOU STUPID. AND IT'LL WEAKEN YOU.
IT'S HOW DEMONS TAKE HOLD. SHE'S GONE, ZOE. WE HAVE TO STAY STRONG.
WAS MOM WITH DAD IN WHATEVER LIMBO YOU WENT TO?!
...
YES.
GUUHHH...

GLAD WE SAVED YOU... TWICE...

...YOU'RE RIGHT ON TIME TO KILL US.
B-BUT...THE MASSACRE'S OVER.

MASSACRE? LADY, THAT WAS HIGH TEA COMPARED TO THE SHIT THAT'S ABOUT TO GO DOWN.
GRRRR...
RRR...

DIG IN!
OH, CRAP...
GRRRR...
RAWR...
GRRAR...

PLEASE GOD, WORK...
"FLATUS!"

SOFT ONE HAS BITE. ANOTHER YEAR PASSED. YET MORE EDGE.

HOW'D YOU KNOW IT'S MY BIRTHDAY?

WAS A MEAGER CELEBRATION.
I LEFT GIFTS.
TED...?
MY CHILDREN...? YOU?!
GAAAAIL... KEEP COOL.
CONCENTRATE--
I AM.
"INTEREO!"
EXCELLENT.
GGGH
C'MERE BOY!
GUHH..
RAWR...
GAA...

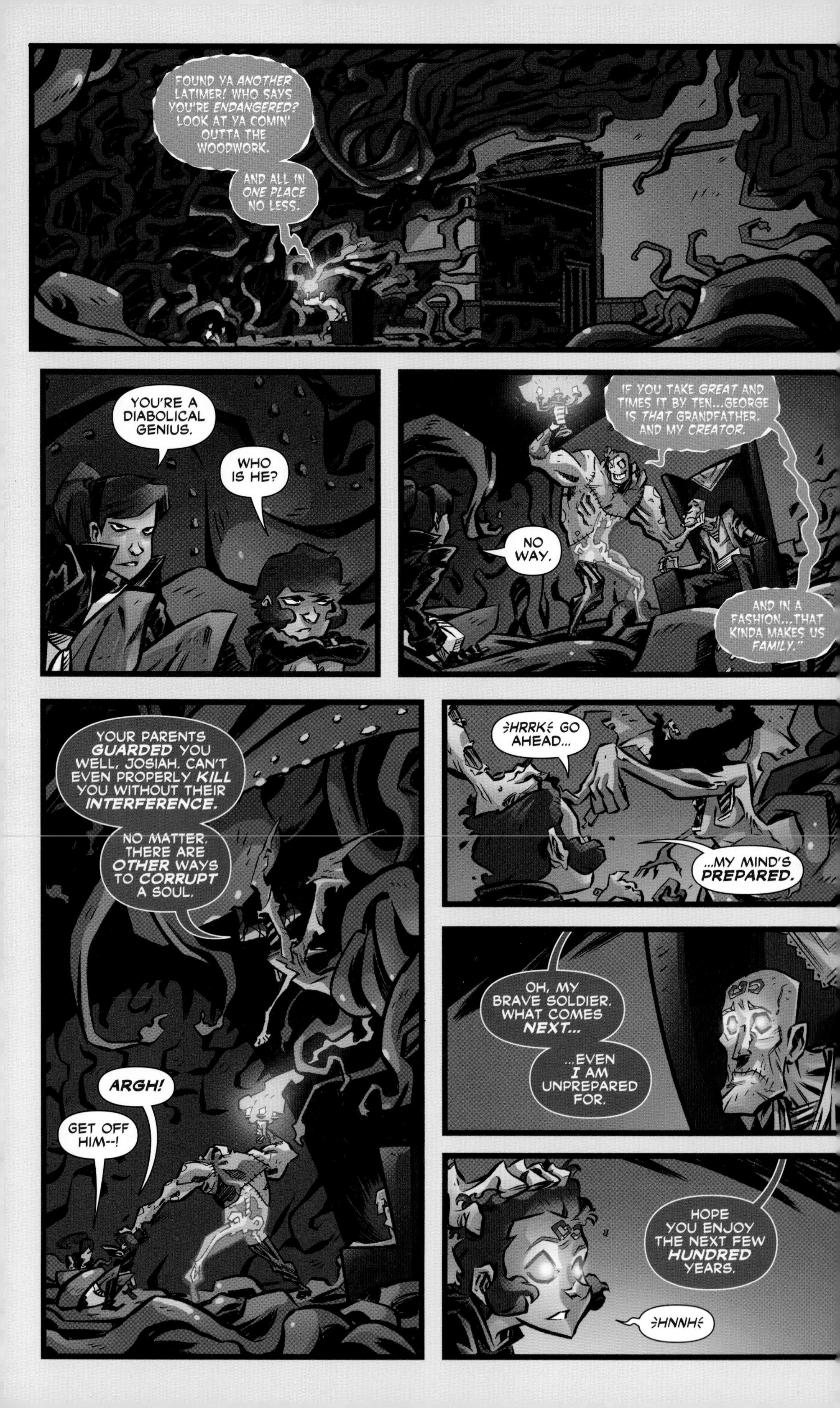
FOUND YA ANOTHER LATIMER! WHO SAYS YOU'RE ENDANGERED? LOOK AT YA COMIN' OUTTA THE WOODWORK.
AND ALL IN ONE PLACE NO LESS.
YOU'RE A DIABOLICAL GENIUS.
WHO IS HE?
IF YOU TAKE GREAT AND TIMES IT BY TEN...GEORGE IS THAT GRANDFATHER. AND MY CREATOR.
NO WAY.
AND IN A FASHION...THAT KINDA MAKES US FAMILY."
YOUR PARENTS GUARDED YOU WELL, JOSIAH. CAN'T EVEN PROPERLY KILL YOU WITHOUT THEIR INTERFERENCE.
NO MATTER. THERE ARE OTHER WAYS TO CORRUPT A SOUL.
ARGH!
GET OFF HIM--!
HRRK GO AHEAD...
...MY MIND'S PREPARED.
OH, MY BRAVE SOLDIER. WHAT COMES NEXT...
...EVEN I AM UNPREPARED FOR.
HOPE YOU ENJOY THE NEXT FEW HUNDRED YEARS.
HNNH

OANOKE COLONY. 1589.
SLORF
SCHLOP
CHEW
≯SIGH≮ WHAT ARE YOU DOING, GEORGE?
≯SNIFF≮ OH LORD-- WHY DO YOU HAUNT ME SO?!
HOW MUCH SACRIFICE DO YOU REQUIRE UNTIL YOU LEAVE ME BE?!
HAUNT YOU? I FIND IT INTRIGUING THAT YOU CAN EVEN SEE ME.
YOU ARE NOT DEATH?
I AM. BUT NOT FOR YOU. IN THIS NEW WORLD, I COME FOR YOUR FALLEN BRETHREN...
...AND NOW IT APPEARS, YOUR FAMILY.
I'M THE DEVIL BORN! NO...! Y-YOU TRICKED ME!
IF YOU SEEK BLAME, LOOK NO FURTHER. THE WINTER IS COLD AND THE FOOD SCARCE. I HAVE WITNESSED MORE FOR LESS.
HEAR ME CLEAR, BRINGER...
I WILL NOT STOP UNTIL I FIND A WAY TO REND YOU FROM EXISTENCE.

JOSEY?! SNAP OUT OF IT--!
HE IS RELIVING THE BIRTH OF A DAMNED SOUL. GEORGE'S FOLLIES...HIS OWN.
AND WITH THE GRIMOIRE, AMMON WILL RISE TO FULFILL HIS DESTINY.
WHY--?! WE DIDN'T CHOOSE THIS!
"THE LATIMER PATH WAS PAVED LONG AGO...EVEN BEFORE TIME ITSELF.
"IN THE EMPTY, THE EARTH WAS FAR FROM VOID.
"THE PRIMORDIAL ROAMED, AND WITH THEM, THE OLD WAYS OF ETERNAL.
"IT WAS ONLY WHEN THEY WERE ABLE TO FORGE DEATH...
"...THAT THEY WERE ABLE TO CREATE LIFE.
"WITH TIME HUMANS ACHIEVED MUCH.
"GREATEST AMONG THEM...THE WRITTEN WORD."
"St. George the "Dragon Slayer

THE BIBLE? QUR'AN? ORIGIN OF SPECIES?
YOU FOUND WAYS TO CREATE YOUR CREATORS. YOU BUILT STORIES INTO SUBJECTIVE REALITY.
SO YOU GOT A WORD FETISH? TAKE THAT BOOK. START A CLUB. AND LET MY BROTHER GO!
"THE GRIMOIRE WAS WRITTEN IN THE BLOOD OF THE EVERLASTING.
"WITH THE ABILITY TO SPREAD CONSCIOUSNESS, BUILD REALITY, AND INFECT MINDS...
"...IT PLANTS SEEDS."
SEEDS THAT CAN ONLY BE WIELDED BY ONE SUCH AS GEORGE.
AND SOON, BY ONE SUCH AS AMMON. WHEN HE RISES, THE GRIMOIRE WILL BE MINE TO CONTROL.
YOU KILLED MY PARENTS...
...MY BROTHER...!
...FOR A STUPID MAGIC BOOK?!

ROANOKE COLONY, 1590.
SLRIPPP MUNCH CRUNCH
THAT WAS QUITE THE TANTRUM, LATIMER.
TO CONQUER DEATH, I SOUGHT SOMETHING OLDER. A SHAMAN OF THE SHAWNEE TAUGHT ME OF THE PRIMORDIAL.
BEAUTIFUL AND HORRIFYING ALL AT ONCE.
DESCRIBE THEM?
CAN'T YOU SEE? THEY WHISPER TO ME OF THE END.
THEY FORSOOK US LONG AGO...THE OTHER SIDE OF A COIN.
HNNHH
LET ME SHOW YOU.
THE POWER OF THE COLONY NOW FLOWS IN ME. I AM TRANSCENDED INTO SOMETHING MORE.
SPLURCH
HURK I-I SEE THEM...
THERE IS BEAUTY IN THE VOID, YES?
HNNK I-IS THIS WHAT IT'S LIKE...?
...TO D-DIE?
WOULDN'T KNOW.
I-I'M SCARED...A-ARE... YOU TO TELL ME A STORY...?
NO...BUT I'LL MAKE YOU ONE.
in the end
AS YOUR END BEGINS, ANOTHER'S BEGINNING ENDS.

HE IS HOME.
WOOSH
HOLY--!
IN THE END, THERE WAS AMMON.
In the end there was
Ammon
AMMON WAS EVERYTHING.
MAGNIFICENT.
WHAT'S HAPPENING TO HIM?!
MY CHILD IS BORN.

AMMON WAS LEGION.

KRAKA THOOOM
WHAT THE HELL?!
KROK
TOO LATE TO GO HOME?
STEP AWAY FROM THE GIRL...!
...I WON'T TELL YOU TWICE!
DON'T--! IT'S JOSIAH!

I-I COULDN'T *PROTECT* HIM...
PLEASE TELL ME YOU'RE *ROLLIN'* ON THE BIG DEMON THING.
GRRR...
AIEEE!
UH... SHOULD I *KEEP* ROLLING?
GRAA!
RAOFRW!
NO--
SKLTCH
FEED

THIS PLACE...BUILT UPON AN ANCIENT DAHKMA...
...I SHALL CALL HOME.
THEN ANOINT IT SO, AMMON MY CHILD.
YES...

BLOOD FOR BLOOD TO BEGIN ANEW. TAKE HER NOW.

RRRGH!
BITCH, LET GO OF ME!

BLOOD FOR BLOOD.
NO, JOSEY! FIGHT IT!

SHOULDA TAKEN THE SHOT...
THIS ISN'T YOU KID--!
DON'T DO THIS!

AND WITH THIS, THE END...
NO! PLEASE, JOSEY! IT'S ME! IT'S ZOE!

PIERCE

AND-- AND...OUR PARENTS!

OUR HOME...! DAD...
...AND MOM!

I'M YOUR MOTHER, AMMON...
NOW DO IT!
NO! YOU'RE A LATIMER...!

YES.
P-PLEASE, JOSIAH... YOU'RE MY BROTHER--!
SHUNK

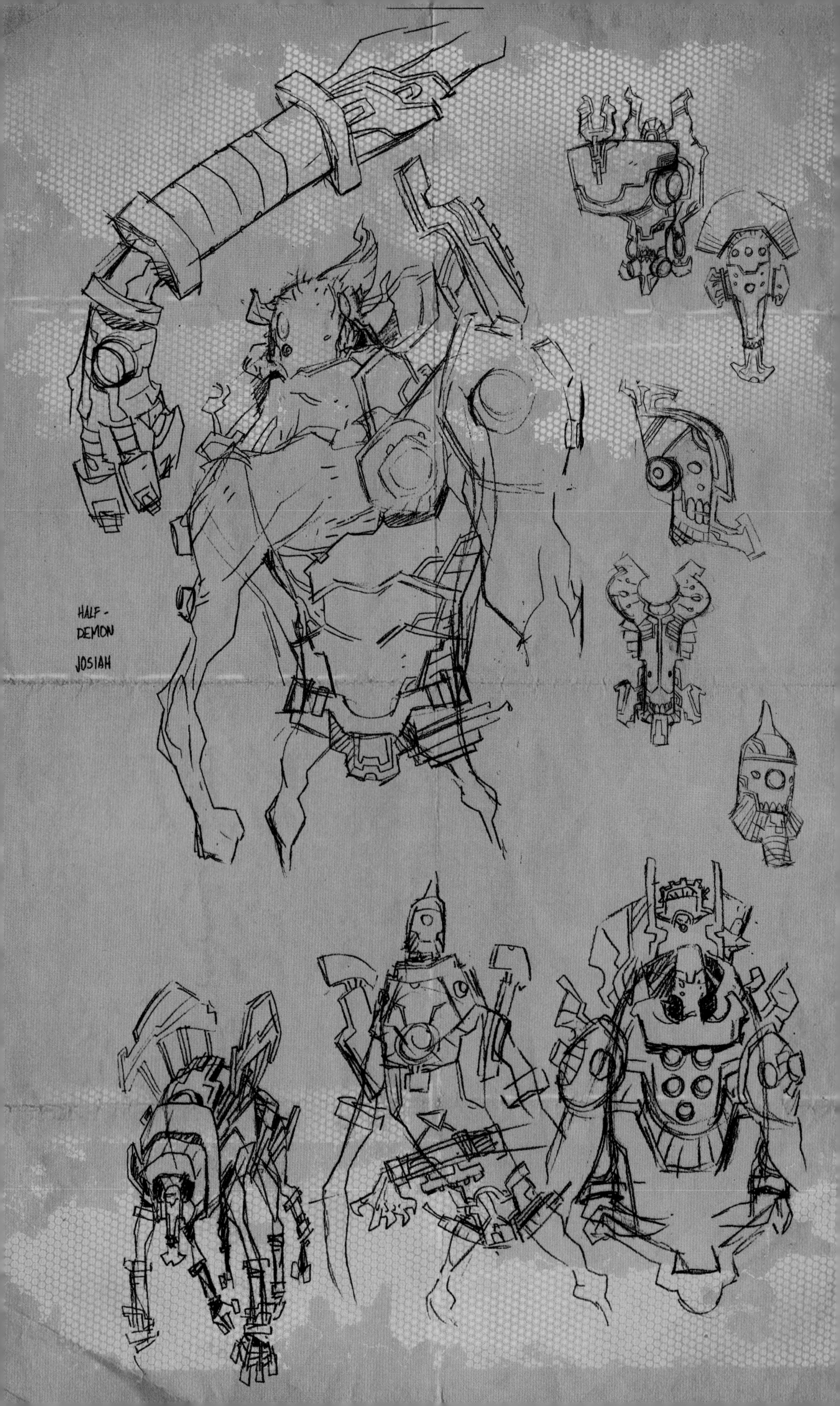
HALF-
DEMON
JOSIAH

THE ALAMO MISSION.
7:54 AM - MARCH 6, 1836.
Always did hate this part.
Being the last in a sea of bodies.
NGHHH...
WELL, HOT DAMN...
...THAT WAS BEAUTIFUL!
No...not the last.
My personal demon is always there to haunt me.
LOOK AT ALL 'DEM BODIES, GEORGIE. SURE MAKES A FELLA HUNGRY!
S-SHUT... Y-YOUR...
HNH?
THE SYMBOLISM... PERFECT.
GREETINGS, GEORGE...

...I AM THE DRAGON.
BUT YOU MAY CALL ME SEPH.
AND WHAT BE YOU, CREATURE?
A PATCHWORK OF THINGS. CREATIONS ARE GIVEN NUMBERS... I AM SEVEN--
--HEY!
G-GO... 'HEAD...T-TAKE IT UP, DEMON. IT'S YOURS.

YOUR NAME CARRIES ON THE WIND, GEORGE. I HAVE LONG SOUGHT YOU... AND YOUR GRIMOIRE.

THE STORY OF CREATION IN ITS PAGES. THE STORY OF ITS END.
I AM NO FOOL. TO TOUCH ITS PAGES MEANS DEATH.

BUT WHAT MAKES YOU SPECIAL? HOW CAN A SIMPLE MORTAL WIELD SUCH POWER?
I-I'M A... LATIMER.
HE'S A WENDIGO...THE FIRST.
MY MY...THE FAINTEST SCENT OF DEMON. THE SEEPING MORTAL WOUND...YET BREATHING.
THE DUALITY INSIDE YOU IS UNLIKE ANYTHING I HAVE EVER WITNESSED.
YOU LOOK FAMISHED.
N-NO!
SHRRIP
I-I BEG YOU...PLEASE! I OVERCAME THIS DEVIL LONG-- MRMMFFF!!
I NOW HAVE ANSWERS, LATIMER DEMON. AND WHILE I CANNOT CONTROL YOU OR THE BOOK...I NOW KNOW WHAT I MUST DO.
MRFGH!
RARHH-- TO THE VOID, FOUL DEMON!
ARRGGH!
QUOVIS

HUFF
HUFF
HUFF...
HNNK
SNIFF

THE RUINS OF BELLWEATHER.
NOW.
=GRRH= AIN'T THIS THE TURN =MRGHH= OF EVENTS? BUT ALL IN ALL, GEORGIE... WHEN ISN'T IT *ABOUT* ME AND YA?
UNTIL THE END.
SHRIFT
THE END.
AHHHH!

YOU'RE MY BROTHER--!
SHUNK
PLIK PLIKPLIKK
YES.
SUCH PRIDE SWELLS IN ME, YOUNG DEARHEART...
?
...YOUR AIM SWIFT HNK AND TRUE.

YOU-- ARE...
...PERFECTION--
WHOOOOOSH
BACK TO HELL, PSYCHO! PTOOIE
ZOE?
JOSEY?
I KNEW YOU WOULDN'T... I KNEW...
WHAT?
I THINK DAD PREPARED ME FOR--UH... ZOE?
WHY'D YOU HAVE TO RUIN THIS?
I'M SORTA-KINDA-NAKED.

MASTER'S DEAD. DON'T YOU HAVE THE GOOD SENSE TO FOLLOW?
HAVEN'T SAID THE MAGIC WORDS.
I LIVED AS GEORGE LATIMER FOR CENTURIES AND I FINALLY RECOGNIZE YOU. CATAHECASSA OF THE SHAWNEE NATION...
MY NAME-- NO!
...YOU. ARE. A SKIN-WALKER!
HE NAKED?
YUP.
HURKK! BLAAARF
HUWACK
RIBBIT!

THIS ISN'T FOR MY FAMILY. THEY WERE BETTER THAN THIS MADNESS. NO...
...THIS IS FOR ME.
SPLURTCH
IT'S OVER...SHIT, I'M TIRED...
YOU GREAT, GAIL.
WE GOT YOU.
MY MIND CAN'T EVEN COMPREHEND THE MOUNTAIN OF PAPERWORK AHEAD OF ME.
SO COLD.
THROW SOME CLOTHES ON, WILL YA?!
FRANCIS!
HEY KID.
LOOKING TALLER.
HOOVES ARE COMING IN.
SIGH TOO SOON.
THOUGHT I WAS LATE...I'M ALWAYS TOO LATE.
WE'RE STILL HERE. YOU WERE PERFECT, FRANCIS.
HERE TO--
LOOK OUT!
FWAASH

FRANCIS?
OH GOD.
T-TO...
...S-SAVE...
NO.
...THE...
...DAY.
CRMMBLE...
KRRK
"SO THIS IS WHAT IT TAKES TO BE A LATIMER?"

SOUND DISAPPOINTED.
JUST THOUGHT THE TRAINING WOULD BE, LIKE, A COOL MONTAGE OF US SPARRING OR LIFTING ROCKS...STUFF LIKE THAT.
Y'KNOW I'VE NEVER BEEN ABLE TO DO A HANDSTAND? ALL MY LIFE. BAD WRISTS. ALL THAT SPELL-CASTING JUJU TAKES A TOLL.
WHY CAN YOU NOW?
PHYSICAL DOESN'T MATTER HERE. AKIN TO DREAM, THE MIND IS THE ONLY POWER! AND LIKE A DREAM, IT IS UNLIKELY FOR A PERSON TO REMEMBER THIS.
YOUR STRONG ABILITY TO RECALL IS A SPARSE FAVOR OFFERED US.
SO I'M HERE TO TEACH YOU THIS.
YOUR SISTER'S THERE TO TEACH YOU THAT.
AND FRANCIS WILL TEACH YOU ABOUT THESE.
HAHA HA!

AHHHH!!
UH...WE NEED TO RUN...
...YOUR MOM'S A DRAGON.
GRRRRRGHHH
THIS IS WHAT YOU WANT?!
YESSSS...
THIS WHAT YOU WANT?
NO.
RIIIP
I'M THE ONLY ONE THAT CAN TOUCH THE GRIMOIRE PAGES WITHOUT DYING! THE ONLY ONE THAT CAN DESTROY IT! IF YOU WANT IT...TAKE ME AND SPARE THEM!
JOSIAH, PLEASE DON'T BARGAIN WITH THE GIANT DRAGON.

FORGIVE THE ROUGH HAND, YOUNG AMMON. AS YOU'VE CAST OFF YOUR DEMONIC SHELL, I'VE CAST OFF MY EARTHLY ONE.
HNK!
JOSIAH! DON'T--!
ZOE--!
STOP!
NO!
THIS IS...

...NOT HOW...

...IT ENDS!

NEVER ONE FOR SENTIMENT... BUT IT IS FITTING THAT A NEW DAY DAWNS.
AND WHAT NEXT? ARMAGEDDON?
PERHAPS IN TIME... BUT NO.
THEN WHY?! WHY THE BOOK?
THE AGE OF DEMONS NEARS ITS END. THANKS TO TH LATIMERS THE LILIN ARE ALL BUT DEAD.
THIS IS LYLE McCARTHY...ANY EYE LEFT IN THE SKY?
THIS IS Z-4.
WRITTEN IN THE BLOOD OF A MALACH HAMAVET...
...SECRETS OF DEATH ARE IMBUED INTO THE PAGES THEMSELVES... THE KEY TO EVERYTHING.
BUT IT'S SO... FRAGILE.
LIKE LIFE.
DO NOT ENGAGE THE DRAGON...IT HAS THE LATIMERS!
GRRAH!
THIS IS GENERAL MASON...BELAY THAT ORDER!
LATIMER KIN OR NO, THAT DRAGON HAS ENTERED U.S. AIRSPACE AND SERVES A CLEAR AND PRESENT THREAT.
BOOM
THOOM
WITH ALL DUE RESPECT--!
NOTHING RESPECTFUL ABOUT THIS. FIRE AT WILL!
THWOOM

GRRRRR
CONCENTRATE FIRE AND BRING ME THE DEVIL'S HEAD!
PRECIOUS.
"THE DOME OVER THE CITY HAS DISAPPEARED, MARTY..."
FWOOOOOM
AS MARINES HAVE BEEN EPLOYED TO HANDLE THE SCALATION OF THE KING'S BLUFF MASSACRE."
THE FINAL TOTAL OF LIVES LOST HAS YET TO BE TALLIED, BUT BELIEVED TO BE NEAR TRIPLE DIGITS.
BOOOOOOSH
HOLYSHIT HOLYSHITHOLY SHIT!
BOOM BOOOM
FWOOOSH
"AND MANY-- INCLUDING TWO CHILDREN-- STILL FIGHT FOR THEIR LIVES."

"IT IS ABSOLUTE PANDEMONIUM IN THE SKIES TODAY, ROBERT.
"THE LATIMERS' HOMETOWN OF KING'S BLUFF HAS COME UNDER FIRE EARLY LAST NIGHT...
KA-BOOM
WHOOM
...LEAVING MANY TO QUESTION, "JUST WHEN WILL IT END?"
CAN WE PLEASE GET OFF THIS CRAZY TRAIN?!
ZOE?! WHAT ARE YOU DOING
SAVING YOU... DUH!
I DESERVE THIS! IT'S ALL MY FAULT!
GET AWAY FROM ME BEFORE YOU DIE NEXT!
OHHHHHH CRY ME A RIVER! LOOK AT OUR FAMILY! WHICH OF US HAS EVER SEEN OLD AGE?! IT'S NOT IN OUR CARDS...NOT IN OUR NATURE!
SO SNAP OUT OF THE "WOE IS ME" ROUTINE AND GIVE ME YOUR DAMN HAND!
FWOOSH
FTOOM
AND AFTER THE TRAGIC LOSS OF RALEIGH AND EVELYN LATIMER, IT APPEARS THAT THEIR CHILDREN, ZOE AND JOSIAH LATIMER, ARE NEXT.
A HARROWING NIGHT AS THE TERRORS HAVE CAST THE FAMILY IN ITS SIGHTS.
WE MAY BE WITNESSING THE END OF A DYNASTY, ROBERT.

BA-DOOM
ROOAAARGHHH!
"SO I WON'T REMEMBER YOU...? REMEMBER THIS?"
"IN TIME IT WILL FADE."
UNTIL WE MEET AGAIN.
≶SNFF≶
KRASH
≶KOFF≶! ZOE?
≶KAFF≶! WHAT?
THINK I CRAPPED MY TURTLENECK.
DITTO.

YOU REMEMBER HOW TO GET OUT OF THIS MAZE?
SAME EVERY YEAR...GO STRAIGHT.
THE GRIMOIRE!
GRRA! WE NEED TO HIDE IT-- URAGHH!
ONLY A HALF-DEMON HALF-LATIMER CAN HOLD IT.
BUT IT'S JUST LEATHER AND PAPER.
LEATHER'S NOT THE PROBLEM...IT'S THE--
--PAPER...
"YOU HAVE SURVIVED." CUTE.
QUICK! FIND SOMETHING WITH IRON.
IRON? WHY?
YOU HAVE SURVIVED THE PUMPKIN MA
TO PIERCE SEPH'S DEMON DRAGON HIDE.
WILL THE STAKE HOLDING SID THE SCARECROW WORK?

WHUMP
THE PAGES FROM THE BOOK ARE MADE FROM DEATH ITSELF. AND LIKE DEATH'S TOUCH...IT KILLS.
SOOOO...?
SO NOW I'M GONNA JAM IT RIGHT INTO SEPH'S HEART.
BY THROWING IT?
I'M WORKING ON IT...SORT OF...
"SHE'S HEADING FOR US! YOU READY?"
MANOHMAN OHMANOHMAN... THIS IS THE STUPIDEST THING I'VE EVER DONE.
NAH... YOU'VE DONE STUPIDER.
ON THREE?
UH... WAIT... MAYBE NOT--
BOOM
FWACK
THREE.

ZWEEEEEEEEEEE!
BOOOINNNG
SON.
"DEATH ISN'T SOMETHING TO BE AFRAID OF...
"...IT'S WHAT MAKES LIFE WORTH LIVING.
"PLUS...I BELIEVE THE NEXT GREAT ADVENTURE RESIDES IN THE BEYOND."

"BUT--WHAT IF THERE'S..."
...NOTHING WHEN YOU DIE?
C'MON...
JOSIAH...?
YOU GOT...
...THIS!
DAD!
SON.

SEPH...
...I'M NOT YOUR SON.
SHUNK
GRAGHHHHH
KRASH
<--NEVER SEEN ANYTHING LIKE IT-->
*TRANSLATED FROM FRENCH.
<--THE DRAGON HAS FALLEN-->
*TRANSLATED FROM RUSSIAN.
--KING'S BLUFF MASSACRE HAS COME TO AN END--!

JOSIAH?!
JOSIAH?!
I'M 'KAY...OKAY? I'M ALL RIGHT.
WOOF...
SOB
SAID I'M "ALL RIGHT." YOU DON'T HAVE TO CRY.
JUST SHUT UP...
...TEARS SNIFF CAN BE HAPPY.

ZOE AND JOSIAH LATIMER?
HUH?
WHAT IN THE SHIT DID I JUST WITNESS?
MASON
HOW ARE YOU JUST GETTING HERE?
CAN'T GET BOOTS ON THE GROUND UNTIL ORDERED BY THE GOVERNOR.
HE'S DEAD...
YOU SEE MY PREDICAMENT. NOW WHO WOULD CARE TO FILL ME IN?
LAY OFF, MASON...THE KIDS PROBABLY JUST SAVED THE WORLD.
GET READY TO GO LIVE!
ADJUST THE COLOR TEMP--
WE'RE ON!
WE DONE?
FOR NOW.

I WAS WRONG ABOUT *HIM.*
HERE... *FIX IT.*
THANKS, *EZRA.*
ALL RIGHT! GET BACK! *GET BACK!*
GET THAT CAMERA OUT OF MY FACE!
WITH YOUR PARENTS DEAD--?!
JOSIAH! ZOE?!
CARE TO COMMENT ON THE COUNTLESS LIVES LOST?!
WHAT'S NEXT?
WHERE WILL YOU GO?
KEEP MOVING.
DON'T ENGAGE.
WHO WILL YOU BE?!

WHO WILL WE BE?

WE'RE THE LATIMERS.
B+ NEWS
END BOOK ONE

THE FAMILY
LATIMER.

IN JEWISH FOLKLORE, A GOLEM IS A CREATION OF UNFORMED MATERIAL TO CONSTRUCT AN ANIMATED BEING. MANY POINT TO ADAM AS BEING THE FIRST GOLEM AS HE WAS CREATED WITH DUST, MOLDED FROM IT, AND GIVEN LIFE. THESE ANTHROPOMORPHIC CREATURES ARE FASHIONED TO PROTECT AND HAVE BEEN BUILT BY VARIOUS MEANS OVER THE CENTURIES. ONE WAY TO GIVE LIFE TO A GOLEM IS TO WRITE THE WORD "TRUTH" ON ITS FOREHEAD AND ANOTHER IS TO PLACE A *SHEM* (SMALL PARCHMENT) IN THE CREATURE'S MOUTH CONTAINING ONE OF THE NAMES OF GOD. THE ONLY WAY TO KILL A GOLEM IS TO REMOVE THIS KEY ELEMENT FROM THEIR BODY.

Horror Spotlight "Creation"

Throughout time, various religions, regions, and royalty have walked the dark tightrope that is the "Ritual of Creation." Whether for experimentation, to play God, or for protection, these Creations must never be given proper names. Names humanize them and take the power of their purpose away from them. To be human is to take away the singular vision of being. However, this is only one way to corrupt a Creation; another is to pervert the Creation with tainted materials.

WITH BONE-RATTLING MOVEMENT, GLOWING RED EYES AND TRANSLUSCENT SKIN, THE BAKAAK HAS BEEN DESCRIBED AS "DEATH INCARNATE." A VENGEFUL PHANTOM THAT STEMS FROM OJIBWAY TRIBAL MYTHOLOGY, THE BAKAAK ONLY PREYS UPON WARRIORS. USING BLUNT CLUBS, IT FIRST PARALYZES ITS VICTIMS BEFORE DEVOURING ITS HARD-FOUGHT REWARD... THE LIVER.

Ekeks are derived from Filipino mythology as winged bird-like humaoids who search for victims at night. They hunger for flesh and fetal blood and get their name due to the "Ek-Ek-Ek" sound which is often heard when they attack. Something they easily do by producing a faint echo sound, fooling their victims into thinking they are off in the distance when they are actually near by.

HORROR SPOTLIGHT

"CHENOO"

THE STONE GIANTS KNOWN AS THE CHENOO STEM FROM IROQUOIS TRIBAL MYTHOLOGY AND ARE CONSIDERED SACRED CREATURES. CHENOOS FIGHT AMONGST THEMSELVES AND EMPLOY THE NATURE AROUND THEM AS A WEAPON--USING REDWOODS AS CLUBS AND MOUTAINSIDES AS BLUDGEONING STONES--THE CHENOO ARE NOT ONE TO BE CROSSED. HOWEVER, THEY MOSTLY KEEP TO TO THEIR OWN AND CAMOUFLAGE THEMSELVES INTO THE SURROUNDING LANDSCAPE AWAY FROM HUMAN AFFAIRS. BUT ONCE IN A GREAT WHILE, TRIBAL SHAMANS WILL BE ABLE TO FORCE THESE MIGHTY CREATURES TO OBEY THEIR EVERY COMMAND.

Horror Spotlight

"Spirit of Accident"

According to Chinese folklore, a Spirit of Accident range from Wutou gui (headless ghost) to Diao si gui (hanged ghost) and any other accident in-between. These once human spirits have died before their time and have therefore broken the cycle of existence. The only way to reincarnation is to obtain a replacement spirit to take their place. However, this stand in must die in the same manner that befell the Spirit of Accident. Only then will they be set free.

Following Norse mythology, the direct descendents of Loki, and in particular, his son Fenrir, are the evil wolf-like creatures known as Wargs. These beasts are often mistaken to be direct descendants of the lycanthropes of European folklore; but unlike the common werewolf, Wargs are not anthropomorphic and travel mainly in packs with an Alpha at its head. And while the likelihood of surviving an attack from these creatures is poor, a bite or scratch will not "turn" its victim.

ACCORDING TO NAVAJO LORE, ONE MAY ONLY BECOME A SKIN-WALKER AFTER ACHEIVING THE HIGHEST LEVEL OF PRIESTHOOD. ONCE A MEDICINE MAN, THE PRIEST MUST THEN KILL A CLOSE FAMILY MEMBER IN ORDER TO BECOME A SKIN-WALKER. A BEING WITH THE ABILITY TO TRANSFORM INTO ANY ANIMAL IT CHOOSES, THE SKIN-WALKER MUST FIRST WEAR THE PELT OF THE ANIMAL THEY WISH TO BECOME. THE PERVERSION OF SUCH A CREATURE HAS BANNED THE WEARING OF MOST PELTS AMONG NATIVE AMERICAN TRIBES. TO WEAR THE SKIN OF AN ANIMAL IS TO ANNOUNCE THAT YOU ARE A WITCH OF MURDEROUS INTENT.

SINCE THE RECORDED WORD. MANY NAMES HAVE BEEN ATTRIBUTED TO THE EVERLASTING CREATURES, BUT THEY OPERATE ON THEIR OWN ACCORD; FREE FROM A MASTER, THEY SERVE BALANCE...WITHOUT DEATH, THERE WOULD BE NO LIFE.

IN RARE CASES AND FOR REASONS UNKNOWN, THE MALACH HAMAVET HAVE KILLED VICTIMS WITH BUT A TOUCH. LEADING TO A VARIETY OF TALES RANGING FROM BARGAINING FOR ONES LIFE TO BRIBING FOR ONES DEATH.

"MALACH HAMAVET"

URGING LIFE BY CREATING DEATH, NOT MUCH IS KNOWN
BOUT THE BEINGS KNOWN AS THE PRIMORDIAL. LIKE
LL DISCARDED GODS, THE PRIMORDIAL HAVE BEEN REL-
TIVELY FORGOTTEN BY ALL AND LIVE JUST OUT OF SIGHT;
T THAT ETHEREAL PLACE BEFORE
NE'S DEMISE... WAITING.

HORROR SPOTLIGHT

"WENDIGO"

ACCORDING TO INDIGENOUS TRIBAL FOLKLORE, THOSE WHO INDULGED IN EATING HUMAN FLESH WERE AT RISK OF BECOMING A WENDIGO. THIS OFTEN IS ASSOCIATED WITH THE WINTER MONTHS, WHEN SOME WOULD RESORT TO CONSUMING THE BODY OF ANOTHER--IN MANY CASES, FAMILY MEMBERS--IN ORDER TO KEEP FROM STARVING. ONCE THE CANNIBAL CONSUMES FLESH, IT IS BELIEVED THAT THEY OPEN THEMSELVES TO DEMONIC POSSESSION. IN THIS FINAL TRANSFORMATION, THE WENDIGO BECOMES VIOLENT WITH THE SINGULAR

Horror Spotlight

"Succubus"

Spawning out of medieval legend, the Succubus is a female demon that can seduce men with even the strongest of wills, whether for harm, death, or birth. According to the Malleus Maleficarum--a treatise on the prosecution of witches--the Succubus will seduce men in female form to impregnate another female with the help of an Incubus. However, some Succubi are able to possess a female host in order to sire its demon offspring and give birth to a child of Lilith, Agrat Bat Mahlat, Naamah, or Mahalath... Otherwise known as the Four Demon Queens.

SPECIAL THANKS

JACOB SEMAHN

Mom, Dad, and friends for their rad support. Man of Action Entertainment: Joe Casey for all the help and advocating, Joe Kelly for being an amazing sounding board, Duncan Rouleau for the name, logo and laughs, and Steven T. Seagle for the mentorship and career. Everyone over at Image Comics for taking a chance. KFox for the happiness and smiles. Barton for the horror. Erin for bouncing ideas. Lilly for the awesome assistance. Retailers and press for believing in us. The *Goners* team for making dreams reality and distracting me with epic email chains of legend. And last but not least, you the reader—Thanks for picking this up and checking us out.

JORGE CORONA

Gracias a Mamá y Papá por siempre creer. Thanks to Morgan Beem for her support and amazing watercolors. And last but not least, thanks to Jake, for bringing me into this world and the amazing Goners team for making this book what it is.

STEVE WANDS

Donna a.k.a. Mom, my wife Carmela, my sons Jacob and Ethan. The *Goners* team, and to everyone who's getting gone with us.

GABRIEL CASSATA

Parents Michael and Carol, wife Stephanie and my amazing crew of flatters: Stephanie Cassata, Virgel Noserale, Federico Sioc and Warren Montgomery.

MORGAN BEEM

I'd like to thank my family and friends for always being so supportive, and Jorge and Jake for brining me on board. And to all our readers who supported and enjoyed this series.